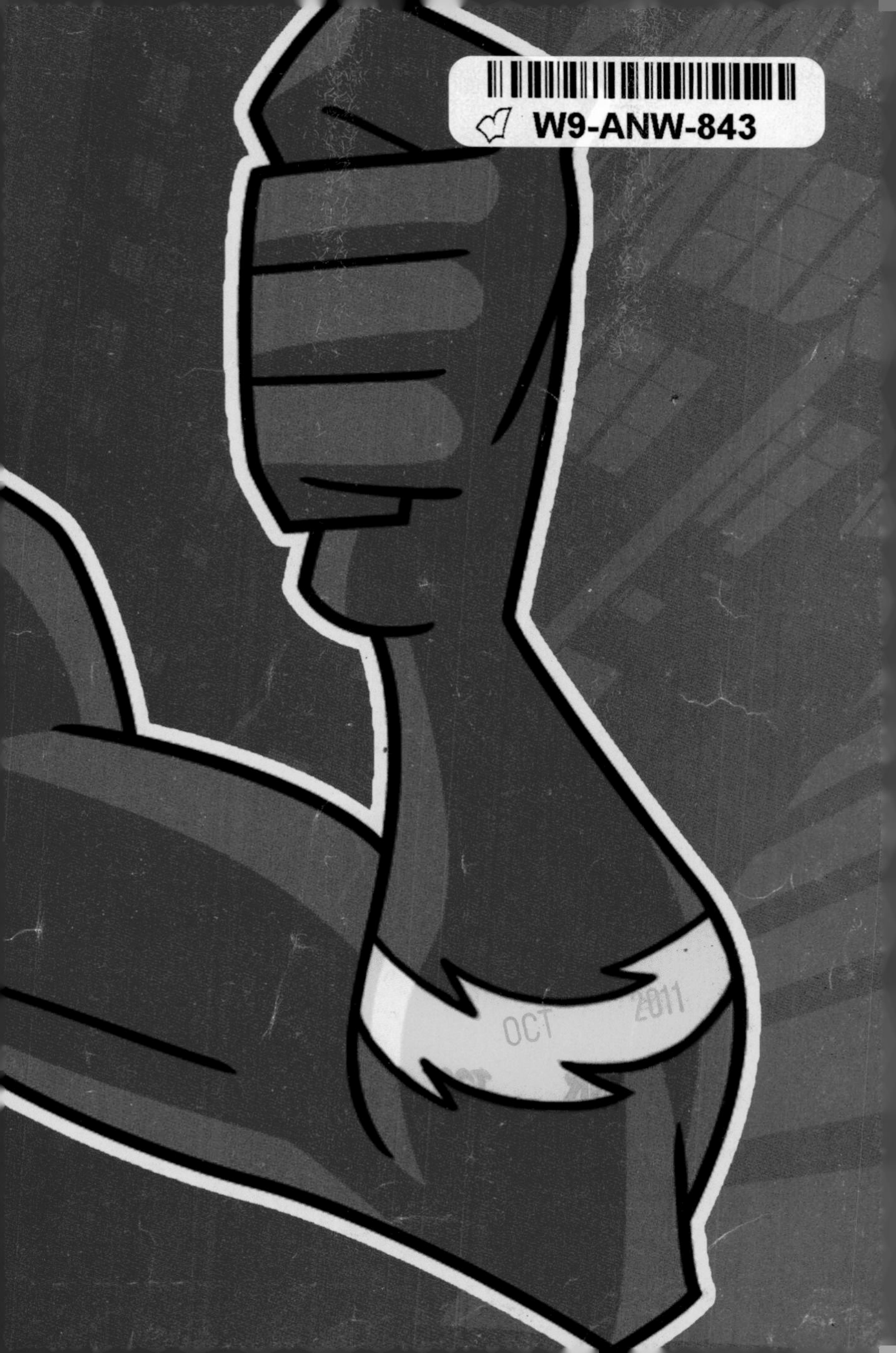

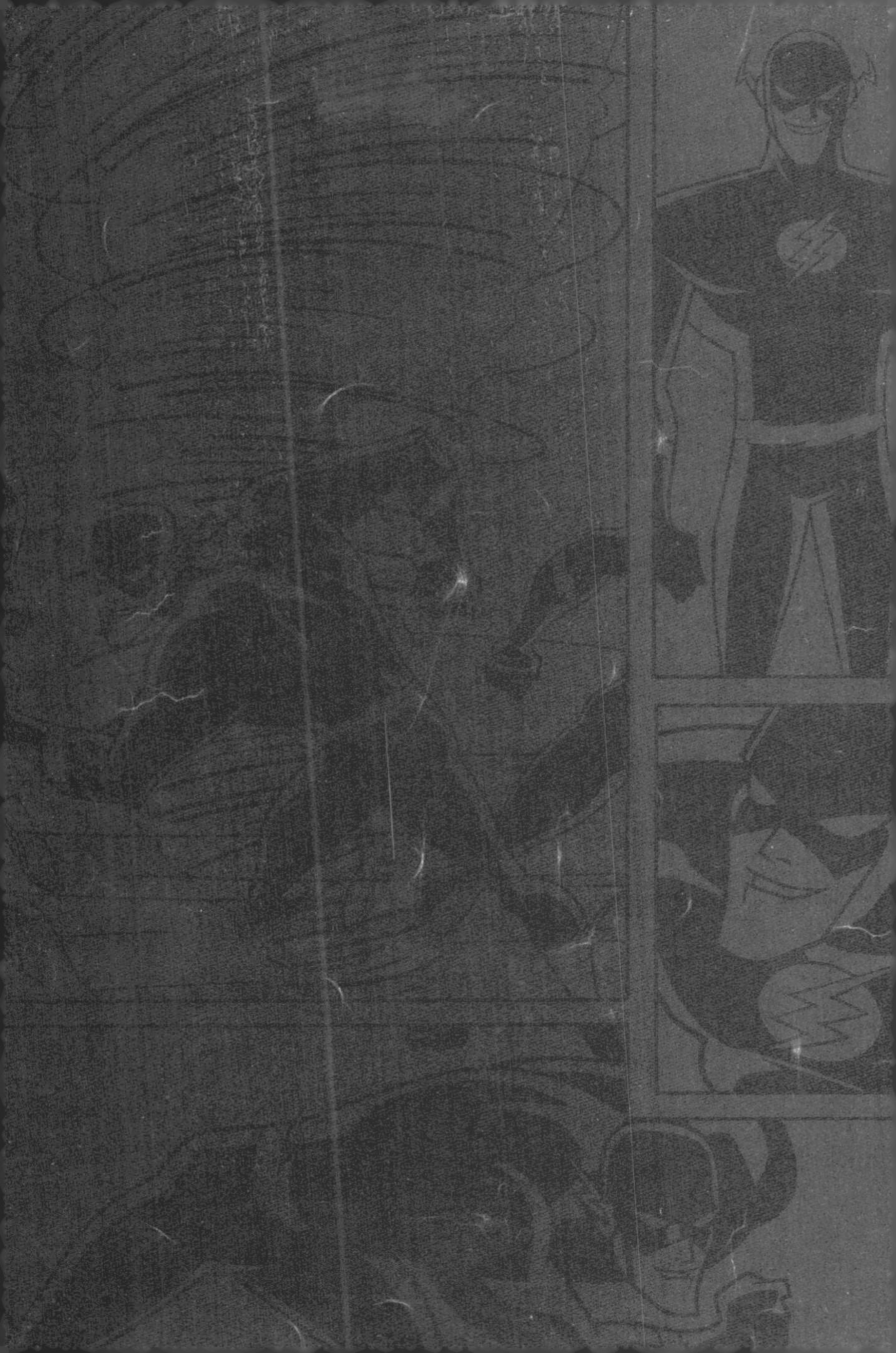

AFTER BEING STRUCK BY A BOLT OF LIGHTNING AND
DOUSED WITH CHEMICALS, POLICE SCIENTIST BARRY
ALLEN BECAME THE FASTEST MAN ON EARTH . . .

SUPER DC HEROES

The FLASH

WRITTEN BY
JANE MASON

ILLUSTRATED BY
ERIK DOESCHER,
MIKE DeCARLO, AND
LEE LOUGHRIDGE

COVER PENCILS BY
DAN SCHOENING

ICE AND FLAME

STONE ARCH BOOKS
a capstone imprint

Published by Stone Arch Books in 2012
A Capstone Imprint
151 Good Counsel Drive, P.O. Box 669
Mankato, Minnesota 56002
www.capstonepub.com

STAR25063

Library of Congress Cataloging-in-Publication Data
Mason, Jane B.
  Ice and flame / written by Jane Mason ; illustrated by Erik Doescher, Mike
DeCarlo, and Lee Loughridge.
    p. cm. -- (DC super heroes)
  ISBN-13: 978-1-4342-2630-3 (library binding)
  ISBN-13: 978-1-4342-3416-2 (pbk.)
  1. Flash (Fictitious character)--Juvenile fiction. 2. Superheroes--Juvenile
fiction. 3. Supervillains--Juvenile fiction. 4. Arctic regions--Juvenile fiction. [1.
Superheroes--Fiction. 2. Supervillains--Fiction. 3. Arctic regions--Fiction.] I.
Doescher, Erik, ill. II. De Carlo, Mike, ill. III. Loughridge, Lee, ill. IV. Title.
  PZ7.M412Ic 2012
  813.54--dc22   2011005146

Summary: Super-villains Heatwave and Captain Cold don't like the Flash,
but they don't like each other either! They face off in a climate-changing
smackdown that could spell disaster for Earth's ecosystems. The Flash tries to
take the foes one-on one, but ends up encased in arctic ice. Unable to move,
Flash watches as Heatwave turns up the threat level by melting the frozen
seabed . . . a sea full of explosive methane gas!

Art Director: Bob Lentz
Designer: Brann Garvey
Production Specialist: Michelle Biedscheid

Printed in the United States of America in Stevens Point, Wisconsin.
032011
006111WZF11

TABLE OF CONTENTS

CHAPTER 1

A FROZEN LAND

Captain Cold stared out at the frozen landscape and grinned. The temperature was 15 degrees below zero. If you added the wind chill, the air felt more like 40 below. Even inside the super-villain's top-secret laboratory, the temps were frigid, at best.

These extremes weren't surprising. After all, Captain Cold was on Icily, a remote island in the one of the coldest places on Earth — the Arctic.

Captain Cold always sought out subzero conditions. For one thing, he hated heat.

For another, the extreme cold kept everyone else away. The frozen felon disliked people as much as he did the heat. That's exactly why he chose the Arctic for his new weapons lab. It was quiet, peaceful, and perfectly chilly.

Carefully carved out of a giant wall of ice, the villain's laboratory was packed with dozens of prototypes and new Cold-Gun equipment. Soon, Captain Cold would unleash these ice weapons on the world!

Outside, the wind howled, but Captain Cold ignored the strange sounds. He was busy perfecting the freezer settings on his new icemaker grenades.

Then, all of a sudden, the wind stopped. A moment later, Captain Cold heard a sound he hadn't heard since he'd arrived on Icily.

TAP! TAP! It was the sound of something dripping.

Captain Cold's eyes narrowed as he peered out his laboratory windows. Everything outside looked the same, and yet the noise continued.

"If something is dripping," shouted Captain Cold. "Then something must be melting!"

The villain's eyes searched the white ground a second time, coming to a halt on a tiny puddle. "What?!" the villain exclaimed. "Nothing melts in the Arctic! It's too cold —"

A bright flash of orange roared across the frozen landscape. It melted a section of ice at the edge of the island.

The tiny puddle grew bigger and bigger. In a matter of moments, the temperature had risen by 20 degrees!

"What's happening?" Captain Cold sputtered.

Suddenly, the icy villain spotted a figure in the distance. The figure had a familiar sneer and showcased a giant flamethrower in his hand.

"Heatwave," grumbled Captain Cold.

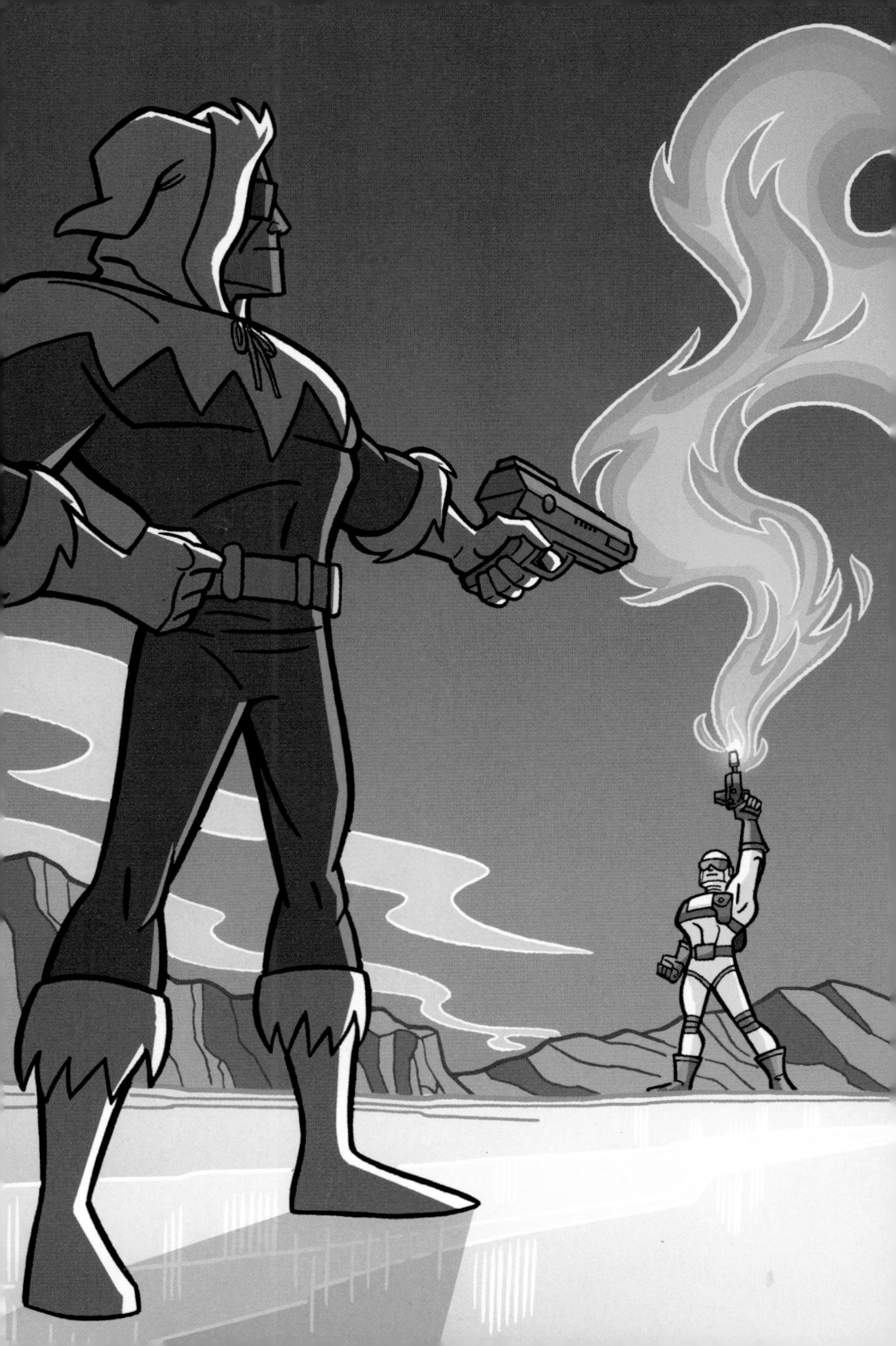

CHAPTER 2

A FIERY FACE-OFF

In an instant, Captain Cold was on his feet. Holding a Cold-Gun at the ready, he raced across the melting snow.

WHOOOOSH! "What's the big idea?" the icy villain shouted, pointing his weapon at his fellow Rogue.

Captain Cold and Heatwave had been known to work together, but only against larger foes like the Flash. When they weren't combating a common rival, anything could happen between them.

Right now, however, the two villains were nothing but enemies.

"Captain Cold," Heatwave said. "I thought I smelled something rotten. What brings you to Icily?"

"The frigid temperatures, of course," Captain Cold replied. "What about you?"

Heatwave stared him down. "A challenge," he answered. "I felt like heating things up a bit, and I thought, why not go to a place that really needs my attention? Someplace . . . frozen." The fiery felon threw back his head and laughed. "I never dreamed that you'd be part of the deal."

Heatwave raised his flamethrower and fired at a section of ice just off the shore, instantly turning it to water. "But I'll consider your presence a bonus," he said.

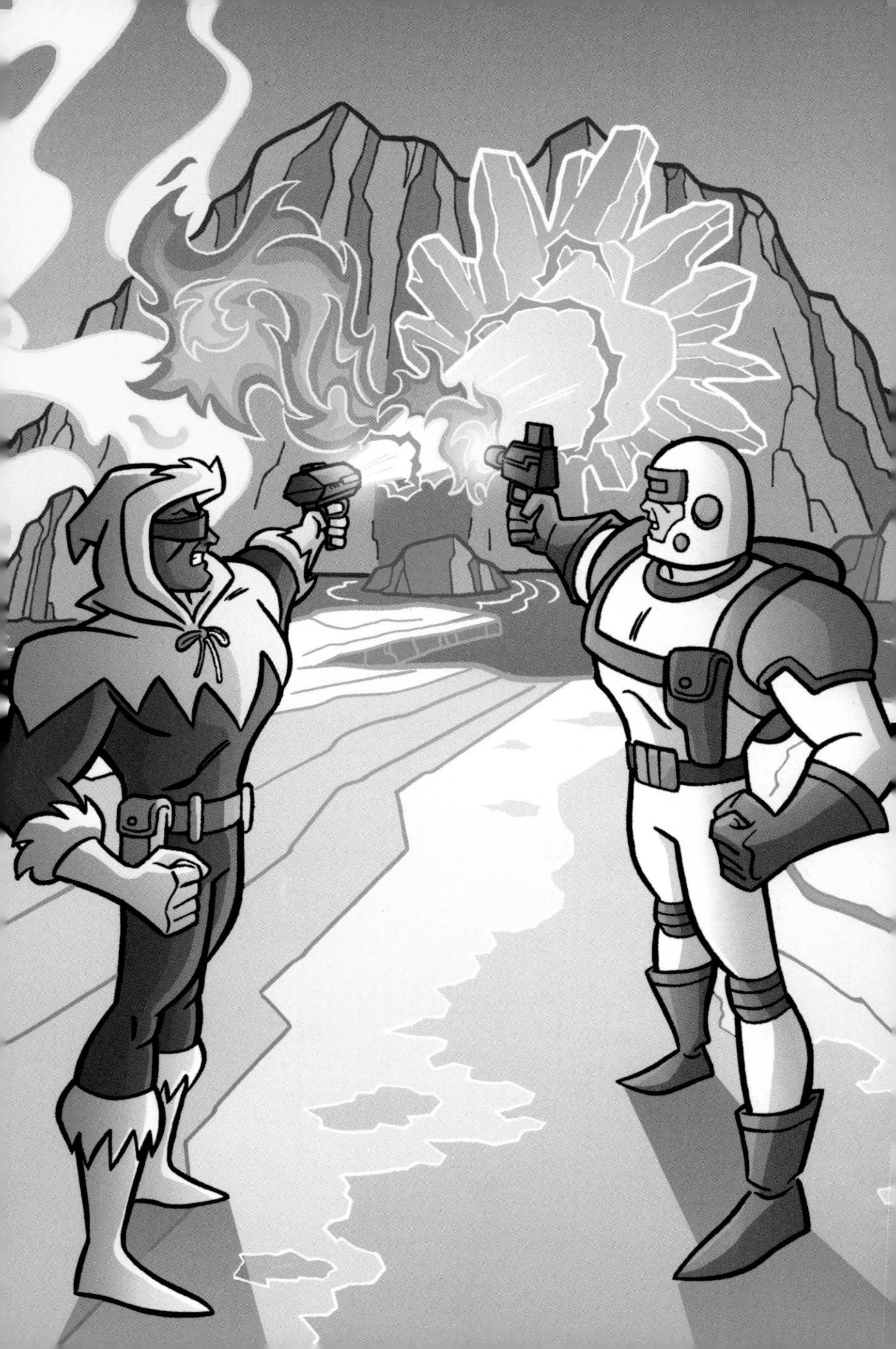

BZZT! Captain Cold fired his Cold-Gun at the area of open water, turning it back to ice. "A bonus?" Captain Cold said with a sneer. "I think you mean the end of your foolish little plan!"

WHOOOOSH! A giant flame shot out of Heatwave's flamethrower. **WHOOOOSH! WHOOOOSH!** Two more. All around them, slushy puddles appeared.

With a quick shot from Captain Cold, ice reappeared where water had been a second ago.

WHOOOOSH! "Fire!" shouted Heatwave.

BZZT! "Ice!" answered Captain Cold.

The two villains battled each other, making the landscape their victim. One second the air was bitter and the land was frozen solid.

A moment later, the temperatures were in the 70s and everything was a melting, muddy mess.

"This is the Arctic!" Captain Cold boomed. "It's supposed to be cold!"

"Says who?" Heatwave asked. "Last time I checked, you didn't rule the world, and you don't control *me*!"

Captain Cold's eyes squinted in anger. He paused for half a second, and then aimed his Cold-Gun at Heatwave. The super-villain didn't usually fire directly at another Rogue, but this was an extreme situation.

"Drop your flamethrower, or I'll freeze you and leave you here for the polar bears," Captain Cold said.

Heatwave roared with laughter, his goggles shaking slightly. "Is that a joke?"

BZZT! Captain Cold fired.

WHOOOSH! Heatwave was ready with his own pull of the trigger.

KA-BOOM!

A wall of fire crashed against a wall of ice, sizzling and crackling in the air. Nothing on Earth could tame these two extremists — except the Flash.

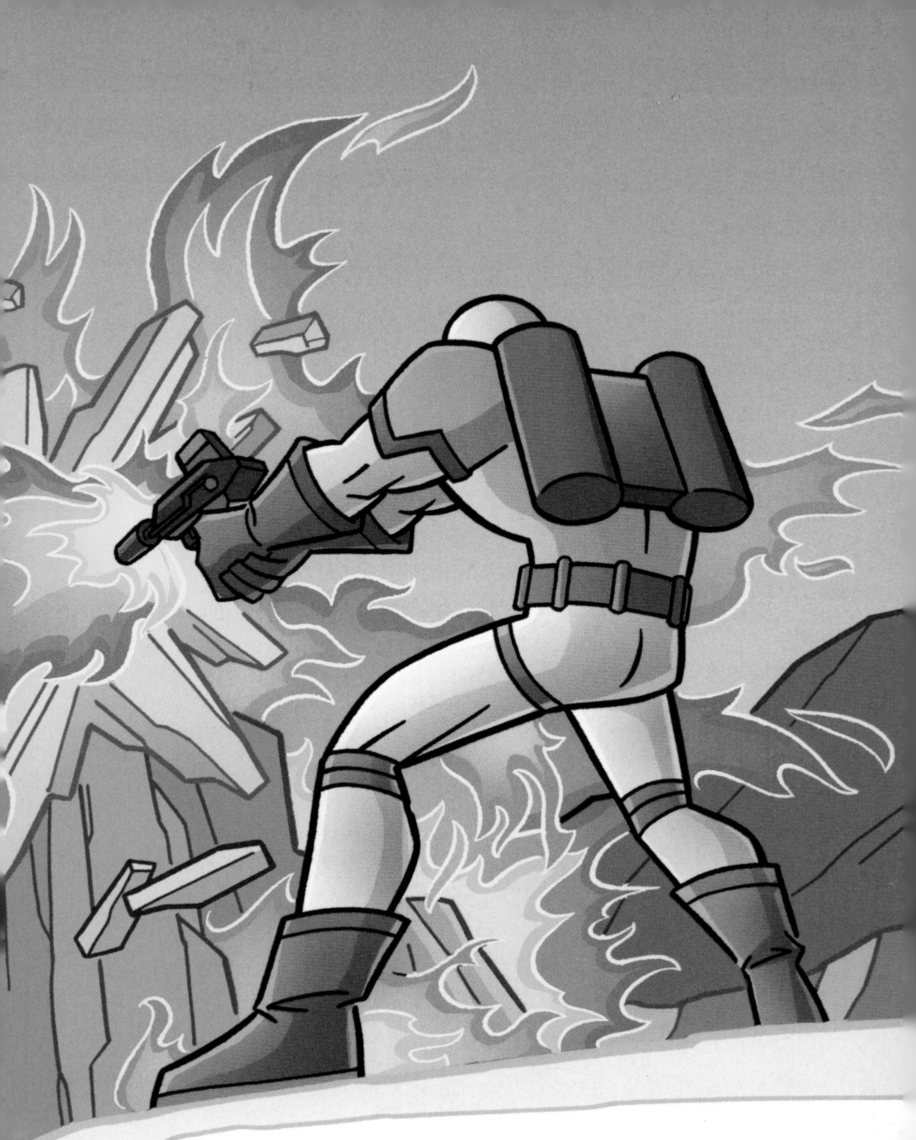

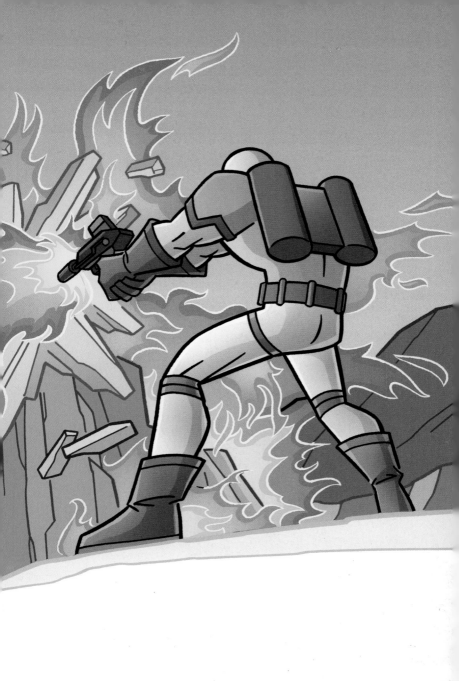

CHAPTER 3

FLASH TO THE RESCUE

In downtown Central City, police scientist Barry Allen passed an electronics store and saw the headlines on a display of flat-screen TVs. "What?!" he shouted, stopping in his tracks.

In big, bold letters, one headline read, "Turbulent Temps in the Arctic!" Live video showed an arctic island called Icily. But it didn't look anything like an arctic island. Parts of the land were frozen. Other parts were melted and slushy.

Barry read the news ticker aloud.

"Strange temperature fluctuations caused by an unknown source," he read. "Historic warming trend spells disaster for the arctic wildlife."

Barry studied the video closely. In the background, he could see some sort of tower of fire and ice. He could also make out the shapes of two figures — one white and one blue — facing off against each other. Barry was pretty sure he recognized the villainous Rogues. As the Fastest Man Alive, the Flash, he'd faced them both many times before.

Barry headed down an alley. Pressing a button on his special ring, the Flash uniform appeared and Barry slipped inside. The red fabric fit him so well it was like a second skin. In less than a single second, the Scarlet Speedster was on the scene.

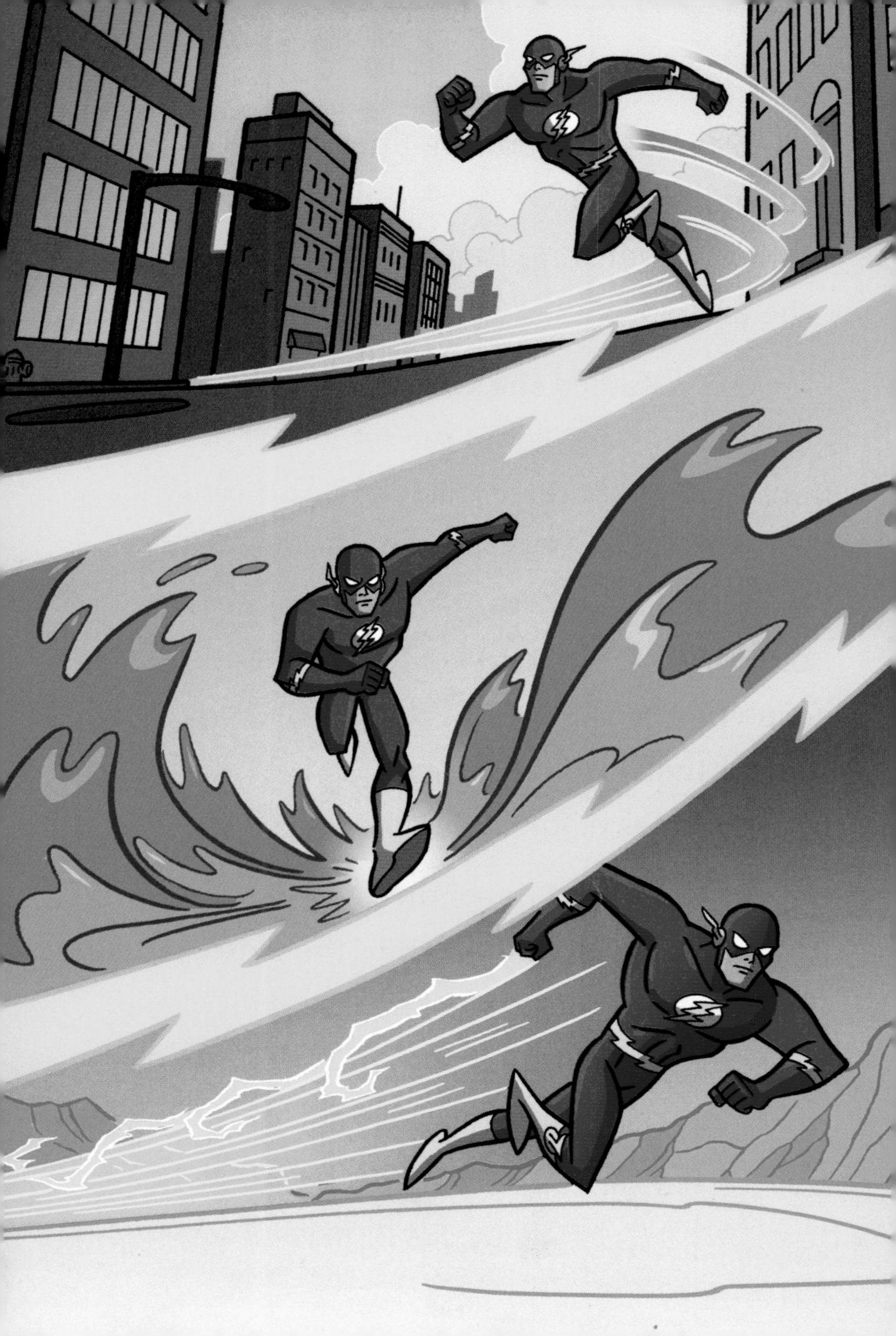

"Icily, here I come!" whispered the super hero. And with that, he took off in a blaze of red. **ZOOOM!**

The Flash roared through the city, out into the countryside, and immediately arrived at the coast. Without hesitating, he sped across the ocean, smoothly and rapidly making his way through massive storms and over rocky islands. The water under his feet got colder and colder, but the hero barely noticed.

Soon, he was sprinting across the ice, creating a red vapor that disappeared into the cold, thin air. Flash had arrived on the arctic island of Icily in record time and wasn't the slightest bit out of breath.

The sight of Captain Cold and Heatwave destroying much of this peaceful arctic land did, however, take his breath away.

The wall of fire and ice was now taller than a two-story building. It stretched as wide as a football field.

"Well, well, if it isn't the scaredy-cat Speedster," Heatwave growled without lowering his flamethrower. "What brings you here? Looking for a little tropical vacation?" He sounded tough, but the Flash could tell that he was tired. The villain's arm shook slightly, and his face was covered in sweat.

"Not exactly," the Flash replied.

"This isn't the tropics!" Captain Cold shouted, shooting at the wall of fire. "Go play your little game on your own turf!"

Captain Cold was no better off. His grimace looked pained, and his aim was not exactly perfect.

Heatwave smirked. "I can assure you, Cold, this is much more than a little game," he said.

"You hothead!" Captain Cold shouted as angry veins popped out of his forehead.

The Flash could see that there was no reasoning with either of them. Still, he had to get them to stop firing at one another. If he didn't, the entire island was going to be destroyed.

The Flash didn't hesitate. The hero moved so fast he was practically invisible. He threw himself right into one end of the fire-ice wall, vibrating like a giant hummingbird. **KRAK!** *Hisssssss* The ice splintered, and the fire sizzled. The Flash vibrated along the wall, ignoring the extreme temperatures.

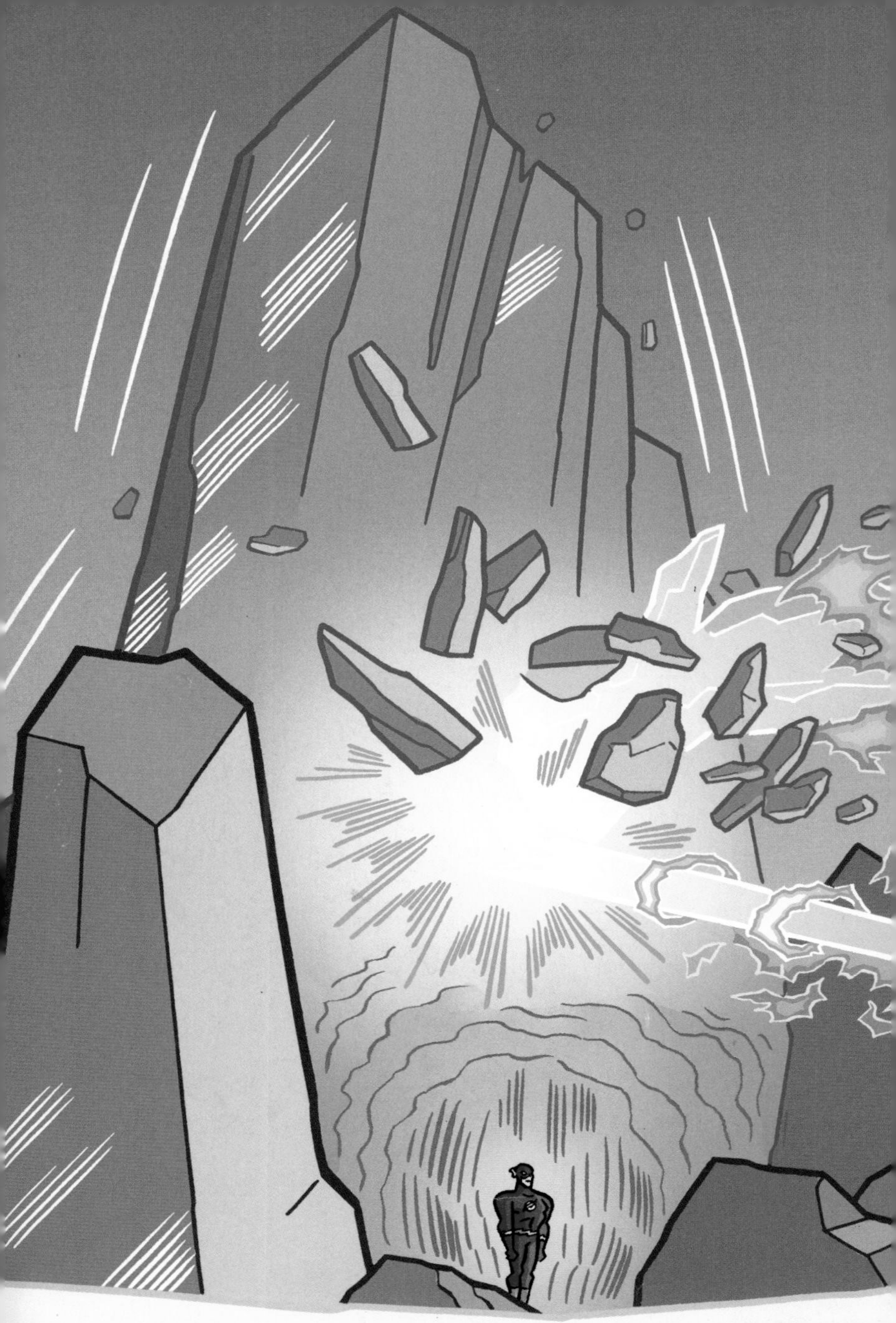

CRUNCH! The ice shattered and the fire expanded backward, sending Heatwave flying through the air and deep into a snowdrift. The blast also disabled Captain Cold's gun.

With Heatwave temporarily out of the picture, Flash and Captain Cold stared at each other. Flash sighed. "Okay, Captain Cold," he said. "I'll give you one chance to explain all this."

CHAPTER 4

THE DEAL

"I was just minding my own business when Heatwave showed up and started making a big mess with his flamethrower," Captain Cold said. "I had no choice but to try to stop him. But now that you're here, we can stop him together!"

The Flash eyed Captain Cold. He knew the evil mastermind couldn't be trusted.

In fact, the last time they had tried to work together, the villain had turned a tropical island into his own personal tundra.

Captain Cold always had a devilish scheme up his sleeve. The icy villain nodded. "I even have a plan," he said.

The Flash tried not to wince. *What kind of plan?* he wondered.

"Don't look so nervous," Captain Cold said with a laugh. "It's not my usual kind of plan. I already told you — I want the Arctic to stay arctic."

The Flash stared hard at Captain Cold. "Just tell me about this plan of yours," he said bluntly.

"Simple," Captain Cold answered. "You just need to distract that weapon-wielding hothead. That will give me time to freeze Icily back to normal, the way it's supposed to be."

The Flash thought this over.

Captain Cold did have the freeze weapons and the knowledge to use them efficiently. Besides, the Flash knew he was up to the task. If anyone could safely distract Heatwave, it was the Fastest Man Alive.

"You want me to be a speed decoy?" the Flash asked.

"Is there a better man for the job?" Captain Cold asked.

"No," the Flash admitted.

"Well, all right then," said Captain Cold, folding his arms over his chest. "Are we a team or not?"

"Team," the Flash agreed. "For now."

*   *   *

"A contest?" Heatwave repeated.

"That's right," the Flash explained. "To test your firing skills. And since I'm unarmed, we're going to agree that you can only fire at me when you have a clear shot. Sound good?"

Heatwave snorted. "I'm in," he said. "And you'll be sorry."

The Flash gave Heatwave a hard look. Then, in an instant, he was gone. A streak of red raced to the southern edge of the island and around a tall, icy peak. Captain Cold was working on freezing everything on the north side of Icily, and the Flash wanted to steer clear so he could make good progress.

THUDDDDMMMMMM!! The Flash moved so fast that he didn't even get wet in the giant puddles — his feet just skimmed across the surface.

Heatwave won't be able to target me when I'm running this fast, Flash thought.

WHOOOOSH! The Flash was suddenly engulfed in a sea of flames. The heat caught him by surprise. The hero thought the first shot would take a little longer. He sped forward, breaking through the fire, and gasped for breath. Heatwave's skills — and aim — had improved since their last encounter.

Up ahead, the Flash could see an icy outcropping covered in long rows of sharp icicles. He sped straight toward it and reached out an arm. He broke the sharp, frozen rods free in an instant. Then the hero grabbed several and hurled them up at Heatwave, knocking his flamethrower to the ground with a clatter.

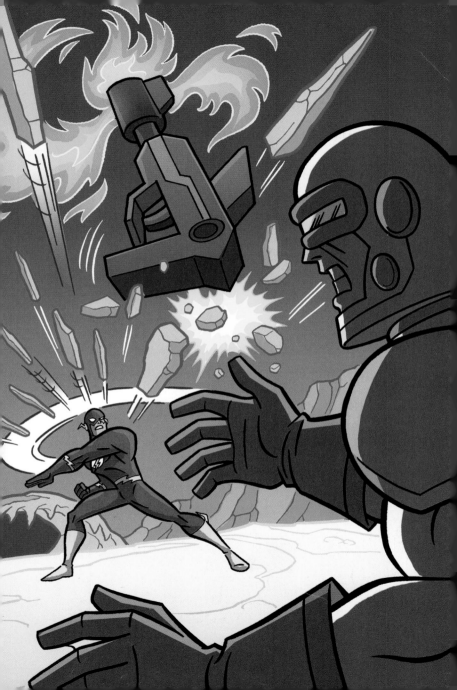

Heatwave looked momentarily surprised and then furious. "Is that the best you got?" he challenged, picking up his gun.

Coming back toward the icicles, the Flash grabbed another armful. This time, Heatwave was ready. The villain fired, transforming the icicles to water in an instant and nearly burning the Flash's arms.

"Nice one!" the Flash shouted. The Flash didn't stop moving as the water evaporated off his suit.

WHOOOOSH! Heatwave fired again, missing the super hero by mere inches.

"What happened to your aim?" the Flash called over his shoulder. "I thought you were a decent shot!" He knew Heatwave had a terrible temper.

The villain's aim wasn't as good when he was angry. "Oh, yeah?" Heatwave roared. "I haven't even warmed up yet!"

WHOOOOSH! A giant wall of flames sprang up between the Flash and the edge of the island.

Whoa! the Flash thought. *That's a pretty big wall of fire.* He roared through it and turned back, using his rapidly moving feet to kick water up and onto the flames. *Pssssstt!* The wall of flames disappeared in a trail of steam.

The Flash looked around. The contest was doing some damage to the landscape, but it was limited to a small area. As long as Captain Cold was successfully freezing the rest of the island, the decoy plan was working.

The Flash sped up a frozen incline to see what was happening on the other side. Barely slowing down to look, he noted that Icily was looking a whole lot colder. In fact, the island almost looked normal again.

"Not bad for a bad guy," the Flash said, watching Captain Cold fire his ice gun at a small pond of water. *Psssssttttt! Pssssssttttt!* It was frozen solid.

WHOOOOSH! The Flash felt something scorch his back.

"Gotcha!" Heatwave cried, hoisting his flamethrower a little higher. "It was only a matter of time!"

The Flash knew his suit wouldn't burn. It was made to withstand intense heat. But having fire shot at his back was still pretty uncomfortable.

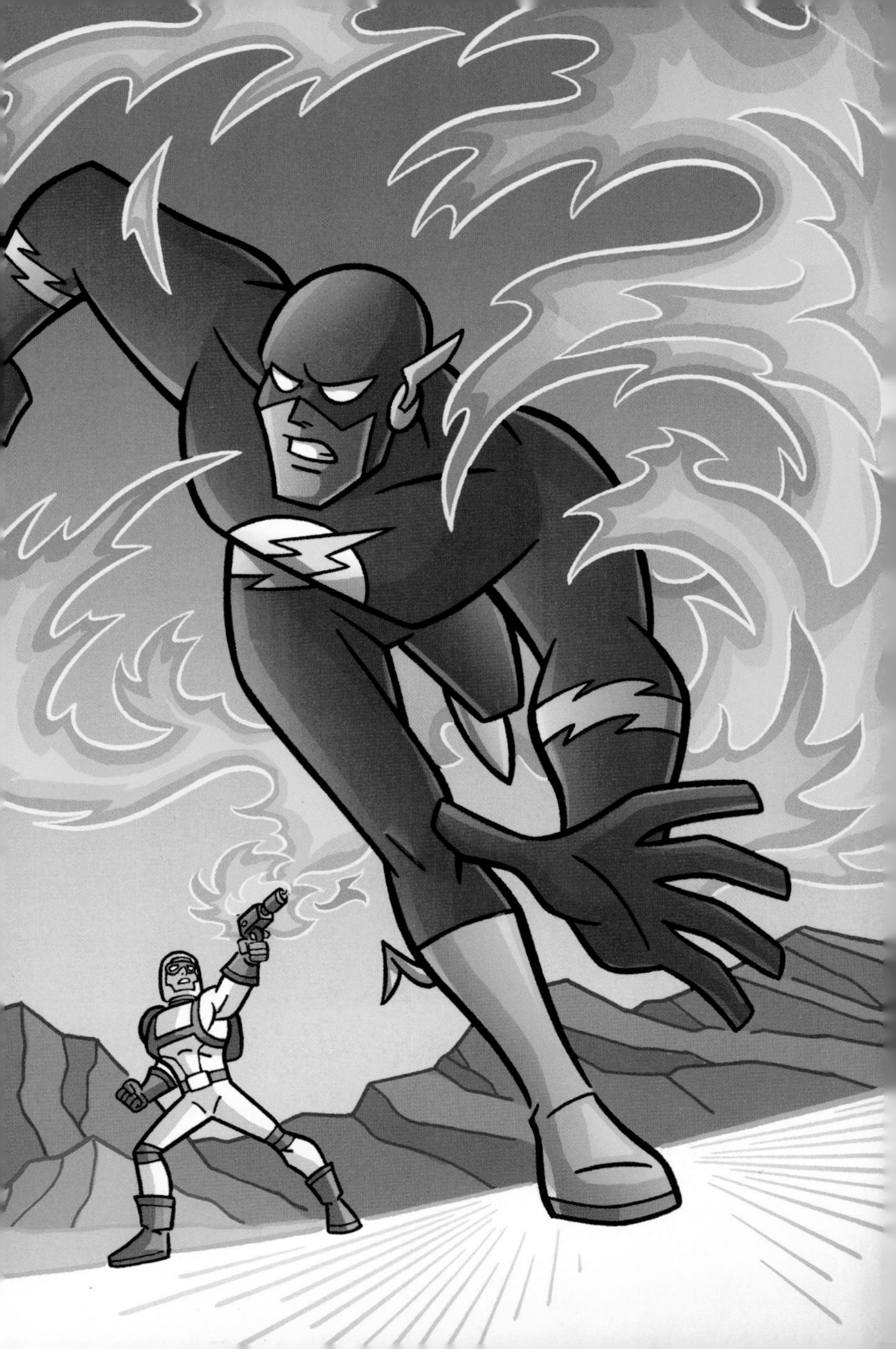

Good thing there was plenty of ice around. In the blink of an eye, the Flash threw himself on the ground, giving his back a good dose of cold.

A nanosecond later, he was on his feet, a blur of red set against the horizon.

THWOOOOMMM!!

The Flash knew he just had to keep Heatwave busy for a little while longer — just enough for Captain Cold to finish his freezing work.

He darted across frozen outcroppings and open spaces at breakneck speed, staying out of sight practically the entire time. Heatwave barely got a shot off, and it was making him mad.

"Quit running away, you coward!" he called out from his icy perch.

The Flash knew that taking a final sizzling hit would be better than ending the match with a furious Heatwave. Flash moved into the open. He slowed down just enough for the villain to fire a shot.

POOF! The fire was blinding, surrounding the Flash on all sides. The hero felt a wave of dizziness. Holding his breath, he lurched forward, freeing himself from the flames and coming to a halt in front of Heatwave.

"Nice one," the Flash said when he'd caught his breath. "I think that tips things in your favor. Match over?" The Flash hated pretending to lose, but he knew that was what it took to bring things to a peaceful end.

"Over?" echoed an icy voice from behind. "Not by a long shot!"

The Flash whirled and saw Captain Cold standing behind them. His Cold-Gun was aimed directly at the Flash's chest.

"I can see the headlines now," the cold crook cackled. "Scarlet Speedster Tricked by Captain Cold." His mouth curved into an evil smile. "Thanks for your help, Flash," he said calmly. "Now freeze!"

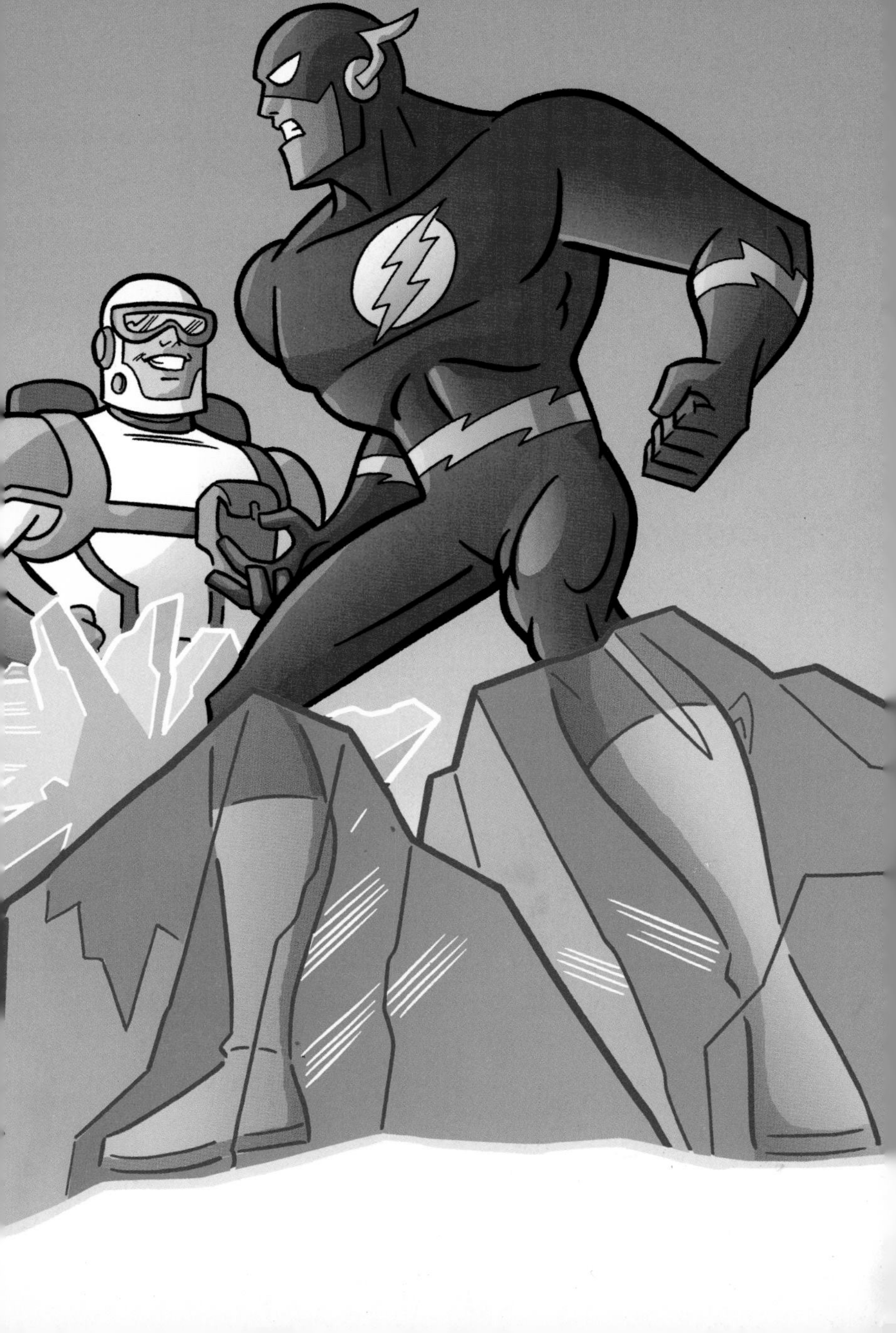

CHAPTER 5

THE BITTER END

Flash's feet were covered in an extra thick sheet of ice. **CRAAAAACK!!** The Flash quickly broke free, but lost his balance and landed on his back.

Captain Cold trapped the Scarlet Speedster with his boot and stared down at him. His weapon was cocked and ready to fire. "Game over," said the villain.

Suddenly, a massive flame shot out of the sea at the edge of the island.

Heatwave tossed his head back and howled madly. "I'm afraid the game is just beginning, gentlemen!" he declared. He fired his flamethrower again, and an even bigger explosion shot out of the frigid sea.

THWOOOOMMM!!

"You're too late to stop me," the fiery felon shouted. "The methane gas has already been released!"

What? The Flash's mind reeled as he tried to grasp what was happening. He'd read about methane gas in the Arctic. It was trapped in the ice beneath the sea, safe from the open air.

But warming up the area released the methane, making it explode and burst into flames above ground. And that would lead to . . .

"A fiery explosion," Heatwave said, as if reading the Flash's mind. "This whole place is going to melt like a cheap candle . . . and destroy the ozone along with it. That'll make this place perfect for me — hot and deadly!"

WHOOOOSH!

Flash looked out at the frozen sea — or what was left of it. Huge towers of flame shot up toward the sky, bursting right through the thinning layers of ice. Large patches of open water were left where a few fires had gone out, with jagged chunks of ice floating aimlessly.

Now the Flash understood. Heatwave hadn't come here on a whim. He'd chosen this area for a reason. He'd come here to release the huge amounts of methane trapped at the bottom of the frozen sea.

The Flash looked up at Captain Cold, meeting his gaze. Captain Cold nodded just slightly, and that was enough. In the face of this terrifying scheme, they had no choice — they were a team once again.

Captain Cold threw his head back and laughed. "Why didn't you tell me what you were up to, Heat?" he asked. "You know I love an evil plan as much as you do."

Heatwave fired another shot. **POOF!** Flames shot fifty feet into the sky!

"I like to keep my genius to myself," he replied. "That way, I will get all the credit."

"Credit? There's enough credit to share," Captain Cold asked. "I want in on the evildoing. How about I keep the Flash right here until you're finished?" He winked at the Scarlet Speedster and fired at his legs.

Flash was frozen to the ground.

"Works for me," Heatwave shouted. He was completely engrossed in lighting the invisible gas on fire.

The Flash looked sideways at the ice surrounding his legs. Thanks to the enormous waves of heat that were coming from the shore, it was already melting. He concentrated on making his torso vibrate so fast it barely moved. A second later, the ice was gone.

WHOOOOSH! There had to be a dozen flaming towers near the shore. The heat was stifling.

"I'll run circles around him until he's confused," the Flash whispered to Captain Cold. "Once he's down, you can freeze him up."

Captain Cold still had his Cold-Gun trained on the Flash's head, but he nodded a tiny nod. His chin was still moving when the Flash sprang to his feet and made a beeline toward Heatwave.

A massive blur of red, he circled the villain once, twice, three times . . .

By the twentieth circle, Heatwave was looking a little dizzy. Exhausted and groggy from breathing in the methane, he collapsed in a heap on the edge of the burning sea.

BZZZZZZZZZZZZZZ

Captain Cold appeared at the Flash's side and fired at the hotheaded crook, freezing him solid.

"Nice work, Cold," the Flash said.

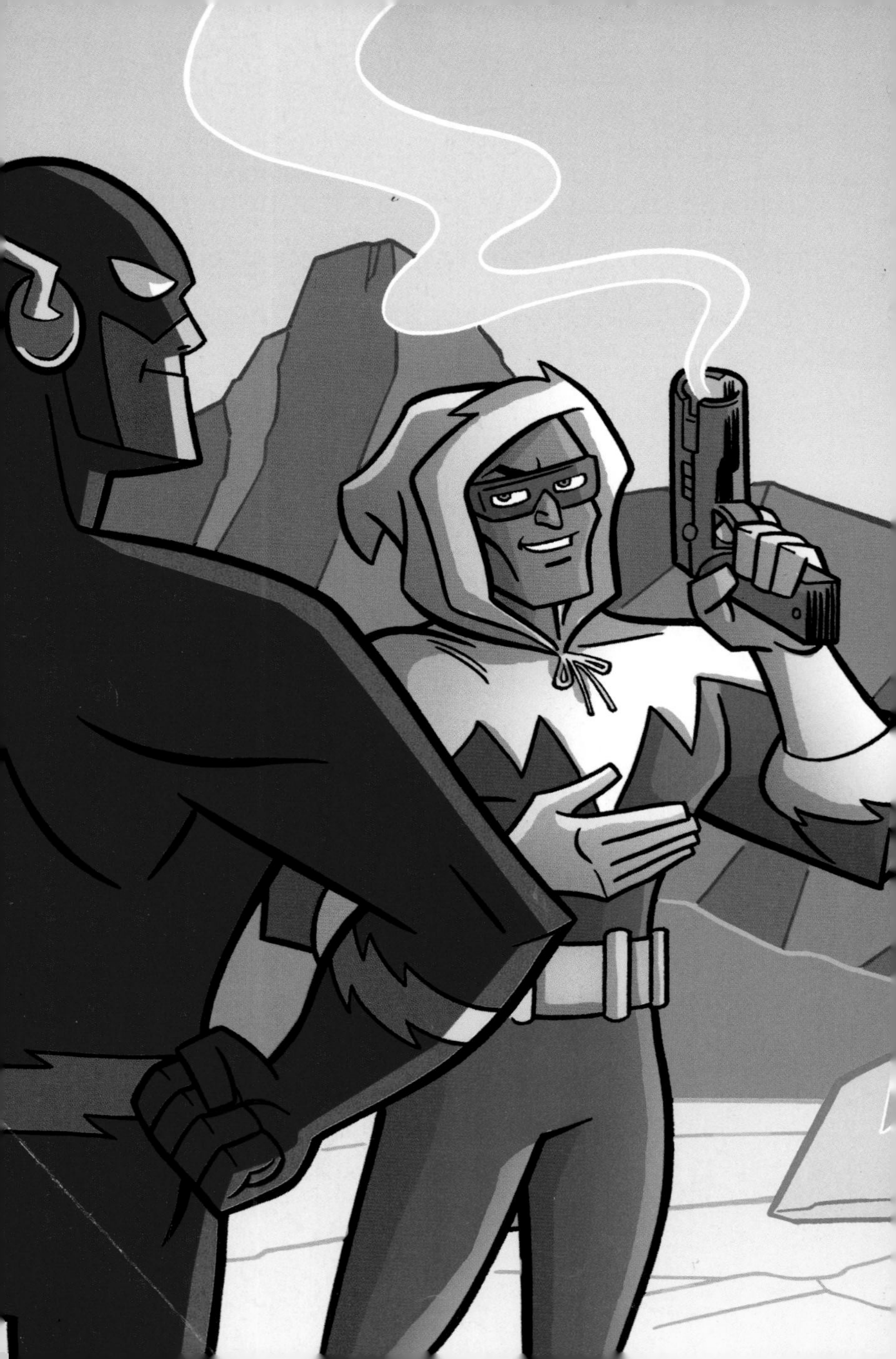

The Flash stared at the frozen Heatwave. Through the layers of ice, he could see that the villain's mouth was contorted into a grimace of surprise.

"Thanks," Captain Cold said to Flash.

The word was barely out of his mouth when the Flash went on another circular sprint. Six, twelve, eighteen speed laps, this time around Captain Cold. When the villain was on the ground, the Scarlet Speedster grabbed his Cold-Gun and pointed it at him. "Hate to do this to you, Cold," he said. "But you've got some wrongs to right yourself. That said, I'm willing to cut you a deal . . . on my terms."

Captain Cold's steely eyes glinted in the blue light. "I'm listening," he said grimly.

"You help me freeze up this section of sea once and for all," said the Flash, "and I'll tell the authorities to go easy on you."

"And if I don't?" Captain Cold asked, curious.

"You'll be looking at the inside of a jail cell — with no air conditioning — for a long, long time," the hero explained.

Captain Cold sighed. He knew he was beat, but he still had one more question. "How easy?" he wanted to know.

"Community service instead of jail time," Flash answered.

"How many hours?" the villain asked.

The Flash tilted his head thoughtfully. "As many as they tell you," he said.

Captain Cold eyed the Cold-Gun in the Flash's hands. "Do I get extra credit for working fast?" he asked, holding out a hand for the weapon.

The Flash stared out at the churning holes in the icy sea. "It can't hurt," he agreed, handing over the gun.

Captain Cold raised his freeze weapon. **BZZT!** He fired at the biggest area of open water near the shore. It froze in an instant. **BZZT!** Another gaping hole disappeared. Captain Cold was working hard — and enjoying himself.

The Flash placed a hand on Captain Cold's shoulder and pointed at the horizon. "You missed a spot," he said with a laugh. The Flash was enjoying it as well.

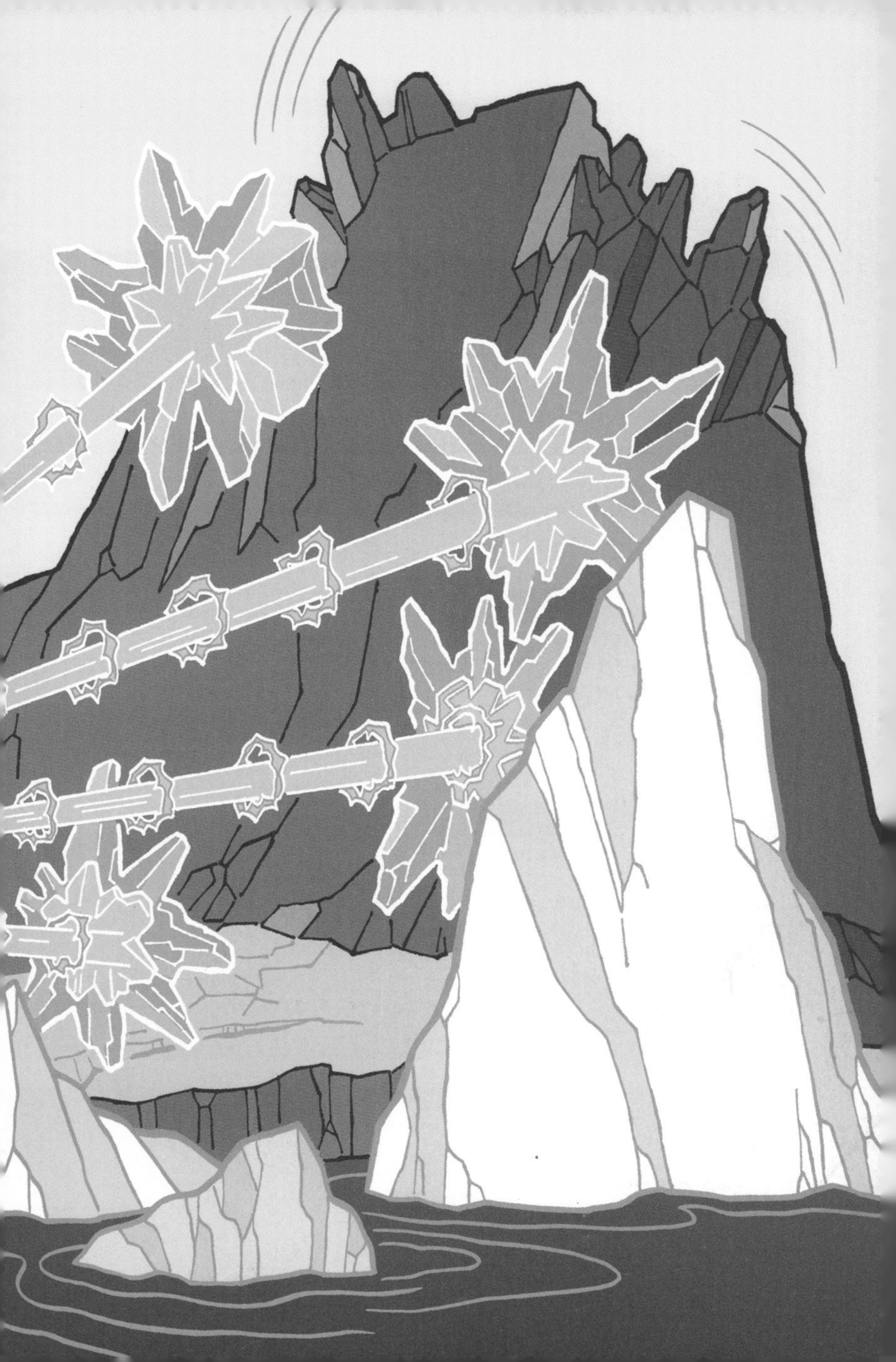

HEATWAVE

REAL NAME: MICK RORY

OCCUPATION: PROFESSIONAL CRIMINAL

HEIGHT: 5' 11"

WEIGHT: 179 LBS.

EYES: BLUE

HAIR: NONE

SPECIAL POWERS/ABILITIES:

Heatwave wields a deadly flamethrower that shoots a stream of fire. His suit protects him from his gun's heat, but he also has a pipe attached to his left arm that functions as a fire extinguisher — just in case.

done

Tue 6:23:12 PM Barry Allen

HEATWAVE BIO

BIOGRAPHY:

Mick Rory has loved starting fires ever since he set his parents' house ablaze. As his home went up in flames, Rory realized he was in some serious trouble. Rather than face his parents' punishment, Mick ran away from home and joined the local circus as a fire eater. However, that job didn't last very long because Mick soon set the circus on fire, too. It was around that time when Mick realized his obsession would serve him well as a super-villain, and the hot-headed, cold-hearted criminal has run wild ever since.

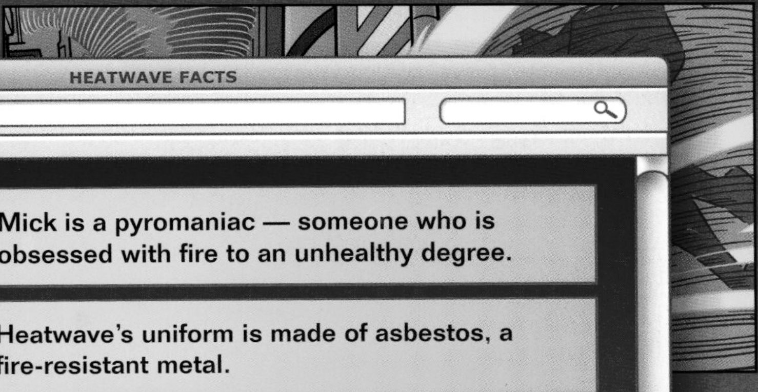

HEATWAVE FACTS

Mick is a pyromaniac — someone who is obsessed with fire to an unhealthy degree.

Heatwave's uniform is made of asbestos, a fire-resistant metal.

Mick has cryophobia, an intense fear of cold, due to being locked inside a freezer as a boy.

BIOGRAPHIES

Jane Mason is no super hero, but having three kids sometimes makes her wish she had superpowers. Jane has written children's books for more than fifteen years and hopes to continue doing so for fifty more. She makes her home in Oakland, California, with her husband, three children, their dog, and a gecko.

Erik Doescher is a freelance illustrator based in Dallas, Texas. He attended the School of Visual Arts in New York City. Erik illustrated for a number of comic studios throughout the 1990s, and then moved to Texas to pursue videogame development and design. However, he has not given up on illustrating his favorite comic book characters.

Mike DeCarlo is a longtime contributor of comic art whose range extends from Batman and Iron Man to Bugs Bunny and Scooby-Doo. He resides in Connecticut with his wife and four children.

Lee Loughridge has been working in comics for more than fifteen years. He currently lives in sunny California in a tent on the beach.

GLOSSARY

decoy (DEE-koi)—something or someone who distracts someone else, or lures them into a trap

extreme (ek-STREEM)—one of two ends or opposites

familiar (fuh-MIL-ur)—if you are familiar with something, you know it well

foes (FOHZ)—enemies

landscape (LAND-skape)—a large area of land that you can view from one place

massive (MASS-iv)—large, heavy, and solid

prototype (PROH-tuh-tipe)—the first version of an invention that tests an idea to see if it will work

rival (RYE-vuhl)—someone you are competing against

rogue (ROHG)—a vicious and dangerous criminal or a dishonest person

tropical (TROP-uh-kuhl)—to do with the hot, rainy area of the tropics

DISCUSSION QUESTIONS

1. Who do you think did more evil things in this story — Heatwave or Captain Cold? Why?

2. Which of the two super-villains in this story do you think would be harder for Flash to defeat?

3. What makes for a real hero? Is it strength? Courage? Superpowers? Discuss your answers.

WRITING PROMPTS

1. The powers of the elements are used by Heatwave and Captain Cold in this book. If you could have one of their powers, which would you choose? What would you do with your new power?

2. Flash is forced to temporarily team up with Captain Cold to fight Heatwave. Have you ever had to work together with someone you didn't like? Write about your cooperative experience.

3. Flash knows it's important to help the environment. What are some ways you can help the world around you? Write down how you can do your part to make the world a better place.

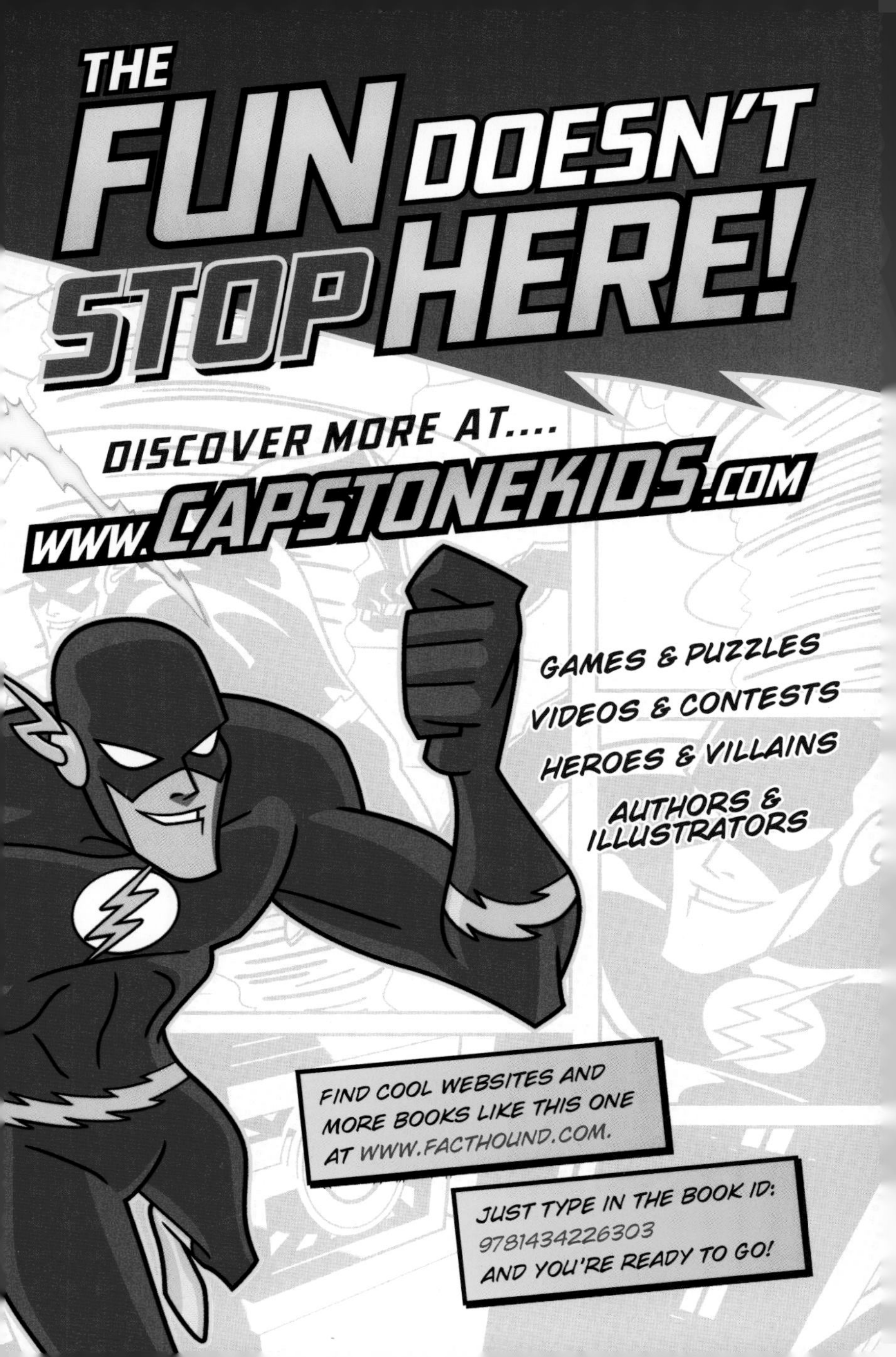
THE FUN DOESN'T STOP HERE!
DISCOVER MORE AT....
WWW.CAPSTONEKIDS.COM
GAMES & PUZZLES
VIDEOS & CONTESTS
HEROES & VILLAINS
AUTHORS & ILLUSTRATORS
FIND COOL WEBSITES AND MORE BOOKS LIKE THIS ONE AT WWW.FACTHOUND.COM.
JUST TYPE IN THE BOOK ID: 9781434226303 AND YOU'RE READY TO GO!

MORE NEW
FLASH
ADVENTURES!

KILLER KALEIDOSCOPE

CLOCK KING'S
TIME BOMB

TRICKSTER'S BUBBLE
TROUBLE

MASTER OF MIRRORS!

CAPTAIN BOOMERANG'S
COMBACK!

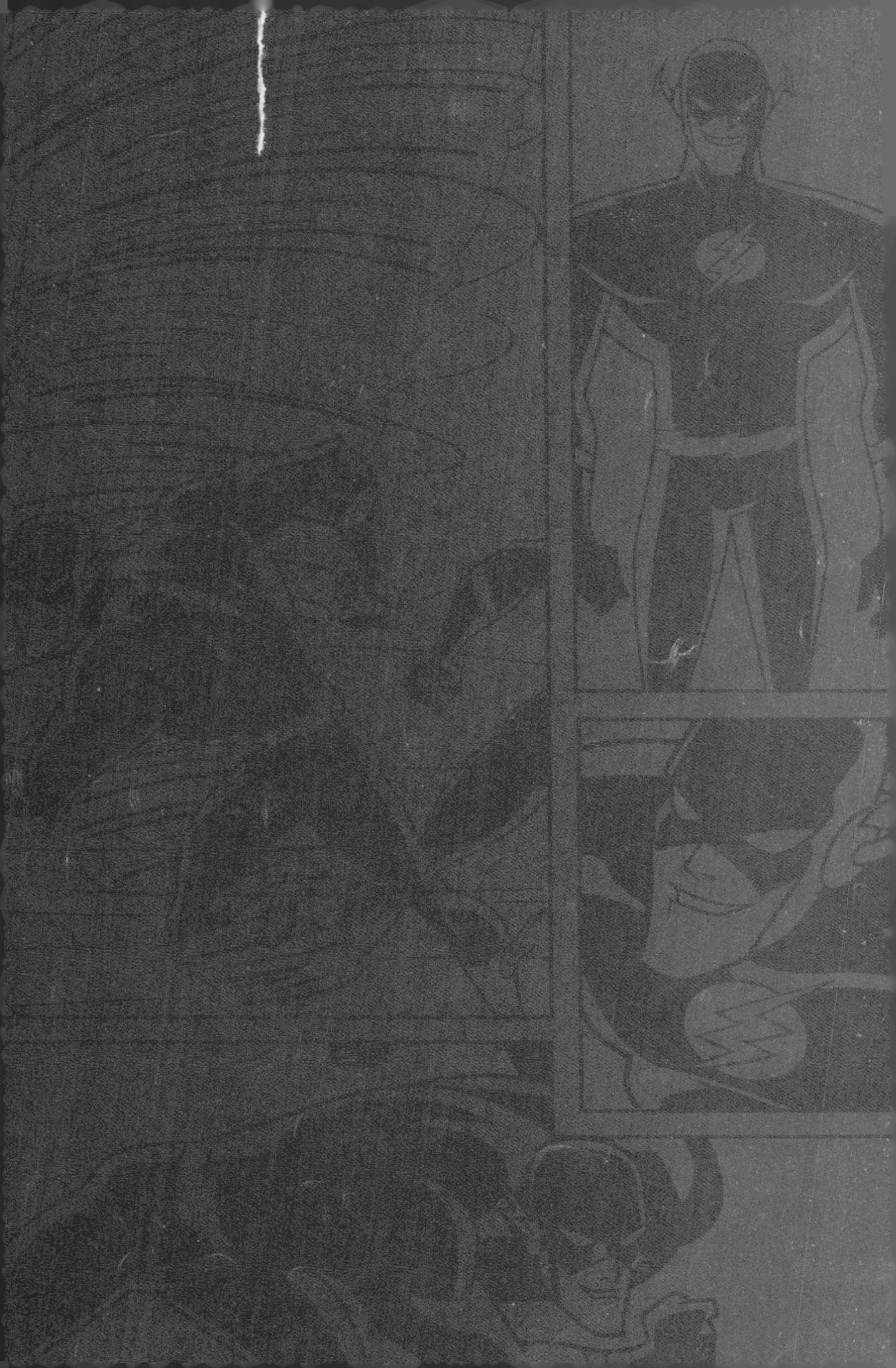

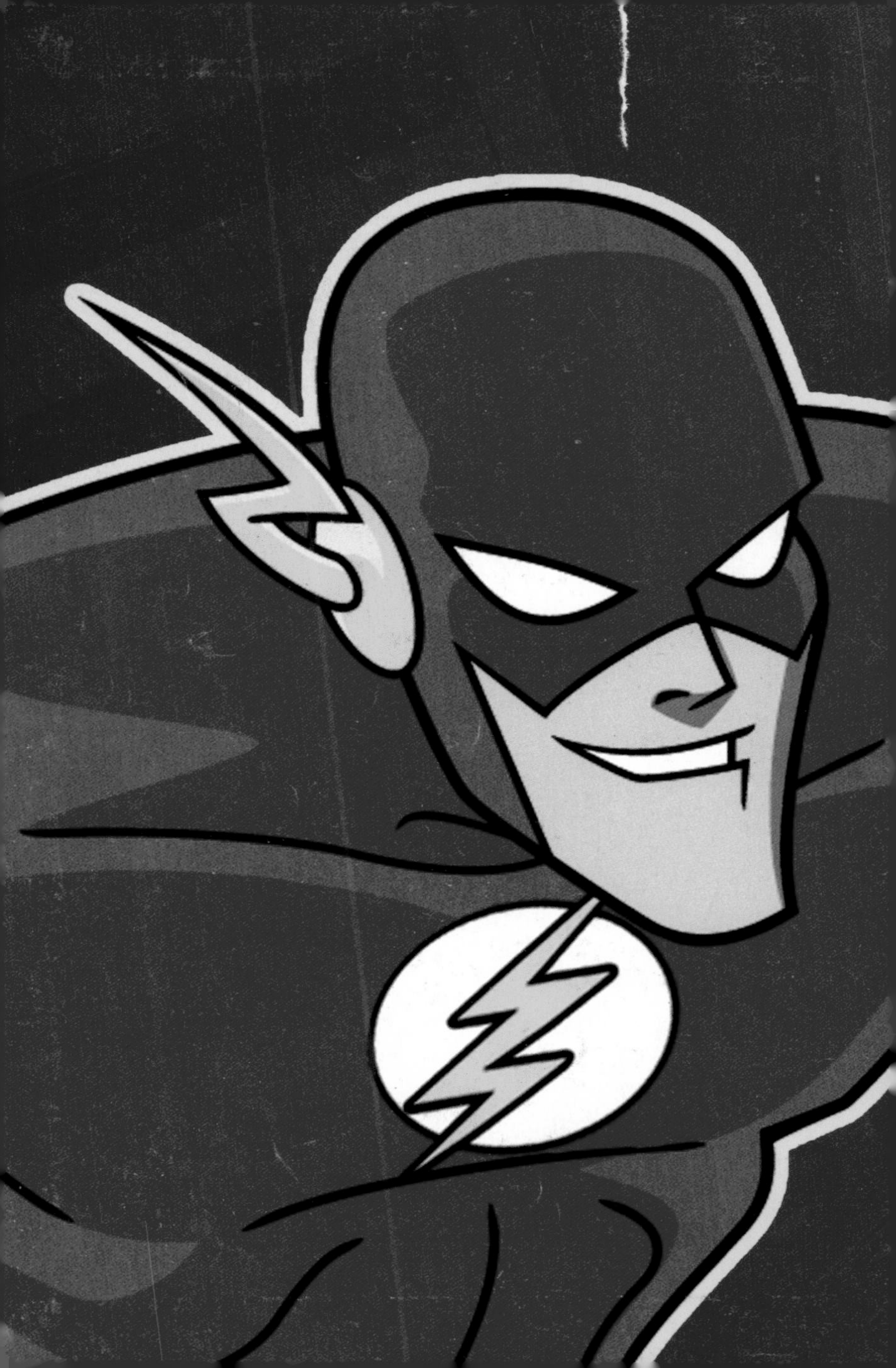